Clovis Crawfish and Fédora Field Mouse

Mary Alice Fontenot

Clovis Crawfish and Fédora Field Mouse

Illustrated by Scott R. Blazek

PELICAN PUBLISHING COMPANY
Gretna

*The word "Pelican" and the depiction of a pelican are trademarks
of Pelican Publishing Company, Inc.,
and are registered in the U.S. Patent and Trademark Office.*

Library of Congress Cataloging-in-Publication Data

Fontenot, Mary Alice.
    Clovis Crawfish and Fédora Field Mouse / Mary Alice Fontenot ;
illustrated by Scott R. Blazek.
        p.   cm.
    Summary: When Fédora Field Mouse is swept away during a hard rain
on the Louisiana bayou, Clovis Crawfish and his friends come to her
rescue.
    ISBN 1-56554-335-1
    [1. Mice—Fiction. 2. Crayfish—Fiction. 3. Bayous—Fiction.
4. Louisiana—Fiction.]   I. Blazek, Scott R., ill. II. Title.
PZ7.F73575Clc 1998
[E]—dc21   97-33394
                                                                CIP
                                                                 AC

Printed in Korea

Published by Pelican Publishing Company, Inc.
1101 Monroe Street, Gretna, Louisiana 70053

For Darrel Landry and Agnes Derouen

Parrain *and* Marraine

of Fédora Field Mouse

It rained and rained and rained. It rained so long and so strong that Clovis Crawfish's mud house melted and ran down the bayou bank in muddy streaks.

Clovis Crawfish didn't care. He needed a new house anyway. The old one was cracked and crumbly. And he liked the rain and the mud.

The rain stopped and the sun came out. Clovis Crawfish wiggled his whiskers and flexed his big, sharp claws. His fan-shaped tail made tracks in the mud on the bayou bank.

"Eh, là-bas, Clovis!" said Théodore Turtle. That means "hey, over there!" in Cajun French.

Clovis Crawfish twirled a whisker. *"Comment les affaires?"* he asked, which is the way Cajuns ask, "How are things with you?"

"Not bad, not bad," answered Théodore. "Except we're going to have a new neighbor, Madame Rat Musqué. She is starting to build herself a house right across the bayou. So be careful! Muskrats eat crawfish!"

"I'm not scared, Théodore," said Clovis Crawfish. "Look at my claws, how big and strong they are. Anyhow, I'll stay on our side of the bayou."

A small tree branch came floating down the bayou. Fédora Field Mouse was clinging to the branch with all four feet and her long tail. She was squeaking and screeching, "I'm drowning! I'm drowning!"

Clovis Crawfish swam out and grabbed the branch with his big left claw. He pulled and yanked until he got the branch and Fédora Field Mouse out of the water.

Fédora Field Mouse was sopping wet and trembling. Her gray fur was slicked down and her teeth were chattering.

"Fédora, how ever did you get in the bayou?" asked Clovis.

"I was on the bayou bank," Fédora said. "I was gathering grass seeds for my children to eat. I slipped in the mud and fell in the bayou, right onto that tree branch."

Fédora Field Mouse began to cry. "My poor little children!" she said. "They must be starving by now!"

Clovis Crawfish wiggled his whiskers. "Where are your children?" he asked. Fédora stopped crying long enough to answer.

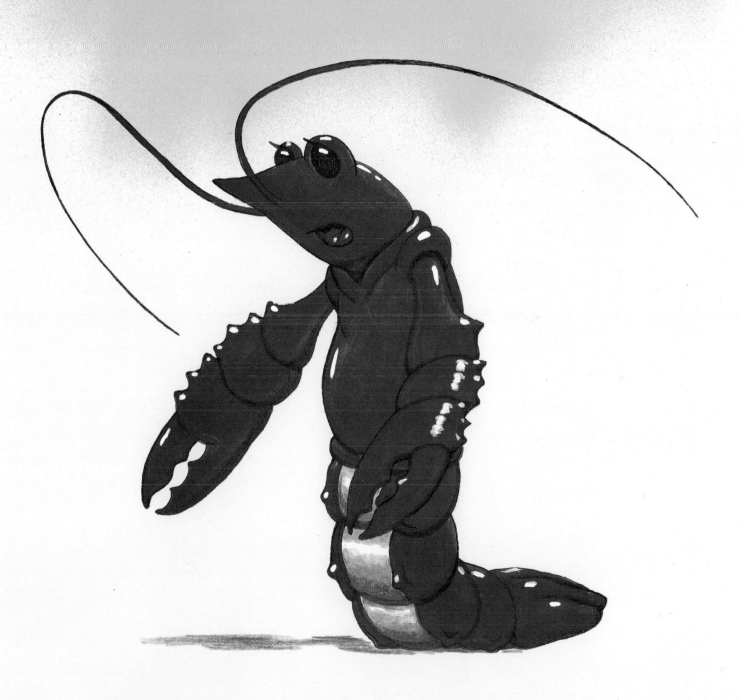

"They're safe," she said, "high and dry in the nest I built for them. They have eaten all the food that I had stored in the hollow tree. There is nothing left but the seed husks."

Clovis Crawfish wiggled his whiskers again. "Come on, Fédora," he said. "Stop crying and help me find something for your children to eat."

Fédora Field Mouse found two acorn cups. Clovis Crawfish held one in each claw while Fédora harvested grass seeds and filled the acorn cups.

Clovis called for Thédore Turtle to help. Théodore pulled up some tender green grasses for Fédora's children. Clovis took them in his claw.

When Fédora, Clovis, and Théodore Turtle got near the nest, one little mouse stuck its head out.

"Mon nom est Félicia," the little mouse said. That means "my name is Felicia." Then she started to cry. *"J'ai peur du tonnerre.* I'm afraid of thunder."

Fédora Field Mouse gave Félicia some grass seeds and tender grass. "Now don't cry," said Fédora. "The storm is all over. See, no more clouds."

Another little mouse popped up. *"Mon nom est Félicien,"* he said. *"J'ai faim!"* That means "I'm hungry!"

Fédora gave Félicien his share of seeds and green grass.

A third little mouse stood up. *"Mon nom est Félix,"* he announced.

"Bonjour, Félix," said Clovis Crawfish.

Félix yawned and said, *"Maman, j'ai sommeil!"* which means "Mama, I'm sleepy!"

Fédora handed out food for Félix. "Eat well, my child. Then you can take a nap," she said.

Mouse number four showed its face. *"Mon nom est Fabien,"* he said. *"J'ai froid!"* That means "I'm cold!"

"Eat this good food," said Fédora. "You will feel better."

"Mon nom est Florence," said mouse number five. *"J'ai chaud!"* That means "I'm hot!"

Théodore Turtle held up an oak leaf. "Here, Florence," he said. "Fan yourself with this leaf."

Florence stopped fanning long enough to eat her dinner.

"*Mon nom est François,*" said little mouse number six. "*Je suis malade,*" he added, which means "I'm sick."

Fédora put a paw on François's head. "You have no fever," she announced. "Here, eat your good dinner."

Just then another little field mouse jumped up. "*Mon nom est Fleurette,*" she said. "*Où est mon dîner?*" That means "where is my dinner?"

Bertile Butterfly flitted by. She stopped long enough to admire Fédora's children. *"Comme ils sont beaux!"* she said, which means "how beautiful they are!"

The Cigale de Bois twins, Chicot and Coteau, made up a song about the little mice.

Translation: *Come with me, right here,*
to see the seven little mice.
The seven mice are very pretty;
they stay quiet and without worry.

Christophe Cricket hopped in. René Rainfrog swung around to the other side of the fern frond so that he could look at Fédora's fine family. Suzanne Squirrel scampered down the trunk of the big oak tree. Fernand Frog climbed up the bayou bank.

Just then Théodore Turtle said, "Oh, my! Look what's happening! Madame Rat Musqué has moved her house over on our side of the bayou. Look! There she is, taking a nap in the sunshine!"

"Let's see if we can encourage Madame Rat Musqué to move again," Clovis said. "All you good friends who have voices—sing! Sing as loudly as you can!"

The Cigale twins buzzed and buzzed. René Rainfrog croaked and croaked. Christophe Cricket rubbed his feet together until his chirping was almost as loud as René Rainfrog's croaking. Fernand Frog bellowed a loud *"Ouaouaron!"*

Madame Rat Musqué put her front paws over her ears. "Stop! Stop! Stop!" she yelled. "You're driving me crazy!"

The singing got louder and louder.

Madame Rat Musqué jumped into the bayou and swam to the other side as fast as she could go.

"Now," said Clovis Crawfish, "I can start building that new mud house."

PRONUNCIATION GUIDE

Cajun-French	English	Approximate English Pronunciation
Fédora	Fedora	fay-dor-ah
là-bas	over there	lah-bah
comment les affaires?	how are things?	co-monh layz af-fair
Madame Rat Musqué	Mrs. Muskrat	mah-dahm rah moos-kay
mon nom est Félicia	my name is Felicia	monh nonh ay fay-lee-see-ah
j'ai peur du tonnerre	I'm afraid of thunder	zhay puhr doo ton-air
mon nom est Félicien	my name is Felicien	monh nonh ay fay-lee-see-ahnh
j'ai faim	I'm hungry	zhay fanh
mon nom est Félix	my name is Felix	monh nonh ay fay-leex
bonjour	hello	bonh-zhoor
Maman, j'ai sommeil	Mama, I'm sleepy	mah-mahnh, zhay so-may
mon nom est Fabien	my name is Fabien	monh nonh ay fab-yahnh
j'ai froid	I'm cold	zhay fwa
mon nom est Florence	my name is Florence	monh nonh ay flor-ahnhs
j'ai chaud	I'm hot	zhay sho
mon nom est François	my name is Francis	monh nonh ay frahnh-swa
je suis malade	I'm sick	zhuh swee mah-lahd
mon nom est Fleurette	my name is Fleurette	monh nonh ay fluhr-et
où est mon dîner?	where is my dinner?	oo ay monh dee-nay
comme ils sont beaux	how beautiful they are	cuhm eel sonh bo
cigale de bois	wood cicada	see-gahl duh bwa
viens avec moi, droit ici	come with me, right here	vee-yanh ah-vec mwa, dwa ee-see
pour voir les sept petites souris	to see the seven little mice	poor vwah lay set puh-teet soo-ree
les sept souris sont très jolies	the seven mice are very pretty	lay set soo-ree sonh tray zho-lee
elles restent tranquilles et sans souci	they stay quiet and without worry	eel rest trahnh-keel ay sahnh soo-see
ouaouaron	frog song	wah-wah-ronh